DARE!
dare
I dare!!!
DaRe!!!
dare!

DARE!

by Erin Frankel

illustrated by Paula Heaphy

free spirit
PUBLISHING®

Acknowledgments

Heartfelt thanks to Judy Galbraith, Meg Bratsch, Steven Hauge, Michelle Lee Lagerroos, and Margie Lisovskis at Free Spirit for their expertise, support, and dedication to making the world a better place for children. Special gratitude to Kelsey, Sofia, and Gabriela for their enthusiasm and ideas during the creation of this book. Appreciation to Naomi Drew for her helpful comments. Thanks also to Alvaro, Thomas, Ann, Paul, Ros, Beth, and all our family and friends for their creative insight and encouragement.

Library of Congress Cataloging-in-Publication Data
Frankel, Erin.
 Dare! / by Erin Frankel ; illustrated by Paula Heaphy.
   p. cm. — (Weird series ; bk. 2)
 ISBN 978-1-57542-399-9 (Hardcover)
 1. Bullying—Juvenile literature. 2. Bullying in schools—Juvenile literature. 3. Fear in children—Juvenile literature.
 4. Courage in children—Juvenile literature. I. Heaphy, Paula. II. Title.
  BF637.B85F726 2012
  302.34'3—dc23

                                                             2012006159

Paperback ISBN: 978-1-57542-439-2
eBook ISBN: 978-1-57542-659-4

Free Spirit Publishing does not have control over or assume responsibility for author or third-party websites and their content.

Reading Level Grade 2; Interest Level Ages 5–9;
Fountas & Pinnell Guided Reading Level M

Edited by Meg Bratsch
Cover and interior design by Michelle Lee Lagerroos
Photo of Erin Frankel by Gabriela Cadahia; photo of Paula Heaphy by Travis Huggett

10 9 8 7 6 5 4 3 2
Printed in Hong Kong
P17200513

Free Spirit Publishing Inc.
Minneapolis, MN
(612) 338-2068
help4kids@freespirit.com
www.freespirit.com

FSC
www.fsc.org
MIX
Paper from
responsible sources
FSC® C018769

Free Spirit offers competitive pricing.
Contact edsales@freespirit.com for pricing information on multiple quantity purchases.

For all children,
young and old, who
have been involved in bullying.

Don't lose sight of who you are.

Know yourself.
Be yourself.

And remember, your brightest
star shines from within.

Hi. My name is Jayla and I'm **scared**.
See that girl? That's Sam. She's tough.

She picked on me a lot last year,
but I never stood up for myself.

I didn't

DARE!

No one else stood up for me, either.
They didn't DARE.

I think I know why.

They've been
bullied, too.

Then one day, Sam started picking on a girl named Luisa instead of me.

"Those boots are weird!"

Luisa's nice. She smiles and laughs and wears what she likes.

4

I felt relieved. I wasn't the one being bullied.
I felt bad for Luisa but good for me.

I **tried** to mind my own business,
but Sam said things to me about Luisa every day.

"Aren't Luisa's boots **weird?**"

"Don't you think she tells the **weirdest** jokes?"

I didn't know what to say. If I didn't agree, she'd bully **me** next.

7

But if I didn't **say** anything, why do I *feel* so bad?

"Stars . . . how lame!"

I remember the way I felt when I was bullied, when no one **DARED** to stand up for me.

I never thought **I** would be the one just standing by.

I was **scared,**
so I took the

DARE!

Now I feel bad for
Luisa and bad for me.
This isn't the kind
of person I want to be.

What can I **do?** What can I **say?**
I take Sam's **DARES** because I'm scared, but then

I feel even
more scared
and alone.

Maybe Sam is
just using me.

"I won't be part of this anymore!"

"Stop it!"

But Sam never stops.
She keeps acting tough
and making DARES.

Maybe she knows that I feel scared?

15

One day when Sam wasn't around, I saw Luisa sitting by herself. Her boots were in the trash.

I wanted to say, "**I'm sorry.**" But the only words I could think of were "**what**" and "**if.**"

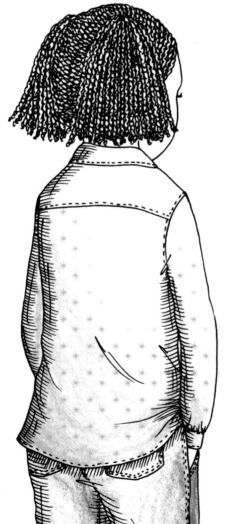

"**What if I talk to Luisa and Sam finds out?**"

"**What if Sam starts calling me a loser again?**"

"**What if things get worse?**"

16

But what could be *worse* than feeling scared all the time? And what have I *lost?*

"My style?"

"My stars?"

"My confidence?"

"My courage?"

"My laughter?"

"My kindness?"

I have lost a lot. So has Luisa. And that isn't fair.

"Let's think of some ways you can stand up for yourself <u>and</u> Luisa."

The truth is there **are** people who care and who **stand up** for others.

19

So, I've been thinking, what about making my own

DARE!

"Tell her how you really feel."

"Stand up and tell Luisa the truth."

20

I still feel scared, but I take the **dare**.

"Luisa, I'm sorry I didn't stand up for you. I found your boots. Do you want to play?"

"Sure!"

I imagine what I will say if Sam finds out
and bullies me.

But now, instead of feeling **scared**, I feel **prepared**.

If everyone joins **together**, we can **all** play a part in making things **better**.

"We don't have to do what Sam says."

"Can you help, Mr. C?"

"We need to talk to the teachers about it."

24

Now Luisa is being **herself** again!

26

When Sam calls her *weird*,
Luisa acts like she doesn't care.
And **I** act like I'm not **scared**.

And **guess what?**
I'm not the only one.

STOP
BULLYING

I discovered something
really amazing!

The more I act like I'm not scared, the more I really don't **feel** scared. It's true!

And the more Sam thinks that I'm not scared, the more she leaves Luisa **and** me alone.

Now that's what I call truth and . . .

Jayla's Notes

Helping Luisa was a *dare* worth taking! Here are some lessons I learned along the way:

Daring to stand up for what's right made me feel good about myself.

Acting like I wasn't scared gave me more courage to help Luisa.

Refusing to take part in the bullying made Sam realize she can't boss me around.

Even when I stood by and did nothing, I knew I was doing something *wrong*.

Luisa's Notes

Jayla helped me realize how important it is to stand up for myself and others, no matter who thinks I'm *weird*. Here are some things I've realized:

When others do nothing while I'm being bullied, I feel sad and alone.

Everyone can imagine how it feels to be picked on.

If I am ever bullied again, I'm going to ask an adult for help right away.

Remember to always believe in yourself, no matter what.

Don't stand by when you see someone being bullied. Stand up and say "Stop!"

Sam's Notes

When everyone stood up together, it was *tough* to keep bullying. Here is what I've discovered about myself:

Telling Jayla what to do made me feel powerful and in control.

One dare leads to another if no one stops me or I don't stop myself.

Understanding how much my behavior hurts people (including me) made me step back and think.

Giving me a choice made me realize I *do* have control—over my own behavior.

Hurting others isn't something I'm proud of, it's just something I do to try to feel good and fit in. (It doesn't work.)

Join Jayla's Courage Club!

I didn't just feel scared around Sam, I *looked* scared. Sam could see that, and it made her feel powerful. So I made some changes in the way I act that made me look (and feel) more courageous. Join my Courage Club and see if you can tell the difference between looking *scared* and looking *courageous*.

Standing up *for* someone often means standing up *to* someone else—which is hard, and sometimes even dangerous. But there are lots of simple and safe ways to stand up for others. Here are some things I did to stand up for Luisa:

★ I refused to take part in Sam's bullying.
★ I encouraged other kids to stand up and help instead of just standing by to watch.
★ I told my parents and teachers about what was happening.*

Can you think of other ways you can stand up for someone? Move over *scared*—here comes *prepared!*

*Telling vs. Tattling
Nobody wants to be a tattletale. But tattling on a person for something small (like picking her nose!) is very *different* from telling an adult when someone needs help. If you were being bullied, you'd want someone to help you, right?

Courage Club: Stop Feeling Bad

I felt bad when I was bullied, bad when I stood by while Luisa was bullied, and bad when I took Sam's dares. Bullying feels all-around *bad*. You can also use words other than *bad* to describe how bullying feels. Want to help me find some?

Here is an example to get you started. The word in the cloud is another word for *bad*.

Example: When I see someone who has bullied me in the past, I feel bad.

When I see someone who has bullied me in the past, I feel **worried**.

Now you try it! Choose a word that describes how you might feel in the following situations. You can pick a word from the clouds or think of your own.

angry   frustrated

scared

sad   lonely

★ When someone gives me a mean look, I feel _____.

★ When I'm being bullied and no one stands up for me,
  I feel _____.

★ When I want to say something to stop bullying but
  the words won't come out, I feel _____.

Courage Club: Start Feeling Great!

I feel great now that I'm standing up to help instead of just standing by to watch. Doing what's right feels all-around *good*. Let's play a feelings game again. This time, find a word that describes how you feel when you stand up for what you believe in.

Here is an example to get you started. The word in the star is another word for *good*.

Example: When I help someone who is being bullied, I feel good.

When I help someone who is being bullied, I feel **proud**.

Now you try it! Choose a word that describes how you feel in the following situations. You can pick a word from the stars or think of your own.

★ When I tell the truth, I feel _____.

★ When someone else stands up for me, I feel _____.

★ When I hold my head up and act like I'm not scared, I feel _____.

Do you want more examples of other words for *bad* and *good*? Ask a friend, teacher, or family member. Then, try out your new feelings words with others.

A Note to Parents, Teachers, and Other Caring Adults

Every day, millions of children are subjected to bullying in the form of name-calling, threats, insults, belittling, taunting, rumors, and racist slurs—and still more are witnesses to it. Verbal bullying, which can begin as early as preschool, accounts for 70 percent of reported bullying and is often a stepping stone to other types of aggression, including physical, relational, and online bullying. As caring adults, how can we help children feel safe, respected, and confident in who they are, and willing to stand up to bullying when they witness it?

We can start by holding children who bully others accountable for their behavior, while modeling and encouraging positive choices. We can provide kids who are targets of bullying with practical coping tools for positive thinking and confidence building. And through stories such as *Dare!,* we can help bystanders explore safe and effective ways to stand up for those who are being bullied and make choices they can feel proud of. We can help children like Jayla realize that when they stand up for others and refuse to join in bullying, they are also standing up for themselves. We can explore practical strategies to help children act on what they know is right, while providing a trusting environment to support their efforts.

Reflection Questions for *Dare!*

The story told in *Dare!* illustrates a fictional situation, but it is one that many kids will likely relate to even if their experiences have been different. Following are some questions and activities to encourage reflection and dialogue as you read *Dare!* Referring to the main characters by name will help children make connections: *Jayla* is a bystander to the bullying, *Luisa* is the target of the bullying, and *Sam* initiates the bullying.

Important: **Online bullying (called *cyberbullying*) is a real threat among elementary-age children, given the increased use of smartphones and computers in school and at home. It's also the most difficult type of bullying to stop, because it's less apparent to onlookers. Be sure to include cyberbullying in all of your discussions about bullying with kids.**

Page 1: Why do you think Jayla feels scared?

Pages 2–3: Why didn't the girl and the boy on page 2 stand up for Jayla? How does it feel to have someone call you names or laugh at you?

Pages 4–5: Why do you think Sam started bullying Luisa instead of Jayla? Why do you think other kids bully?

Pages 6–9: Why doesn't Jayla speak up when Sam bullies Luisa? What are the other characters doing? Why do you think Jayla feels bad? Have you ever stood by while someone was being bullied? What stopped you from speaking up or telling someone? What's the difference between telling and tattling? *(**Note:** See the circle on page 34.)*

Additional discussion questions, activities, and suggestions for the Weird series are available in the free Leader's Guide, which can be downloaded at www.freespirit.com/ weirdLG.

Pages 10–15: What does Sam tell Jayla to do? How does Jayla feel about it? Jayla wonders: "Maybe she knows that I feel scared?" Why would that matter?

Pages 16–19: Why doesn't Jayla apologize to Luisa? After thinking things through, what does Jayla realize? Why are caring adults and classmates important when it comes to bullying? What does it mean to be an "upstander"? *(**Note:** An upstander is a bystander who chooses to stand up for someone who is being bullied or mistreated rather than stand by to watch—which is a form of passive participation in the bullying.)*

Pages 20–23: What does Jayla do with Luisa's boots? How do you think that makes Luisa feel? What does Jayla do to feel more courageous?

Pages 24–27: Is Jayla the only one who stands up for Luisa? What is different about Jayla now? Luisa? Sam?

Pages 28–31: What does Jayla discover?

Overall: Which character in *Dare!* is most like you and why? What would you like to say to this character?

The Weird Series

The Weird series gives readers the opportunity to explore three very different perspectives on bullying: that of a child who is a target of bullying in *Weird!*, that of a bystander to bullying in *Dare!*, and that of a child who initiates bullying in *Tough!* Each book can be used alone or together with the other books in the series to build awareness and engage children in discussions related to bullying and encourage bullying prevention. If you are using the books as a series, consider doing the following activities with young readers.

Series Activity: "I Stand For" Drawing

Discuss with children how standing up for someone means standing up for what we believe is right. Find examples from *Weird!*, *Dare!*, and *Tough!* that show characters standing up for what they believe in, such as Jayla standing up for kindness by giving Luisa her boots back. Ask children to draw a picture of a "stand up" scene and write one word at the top of the drawing to describe what the character is standing up for. When completed, have children share their drawings with the class and tell everyone what they stand for by saying, "My name is _____ and I stand for _____."

Series Activity: Pantomime

Have children pantomime memorable scenes from *Weird!*, *Dare!*, or *Tough!*, while others guess which scene is being depicted from which book.

Series Activity: Caring Constellation

Discuss with children how characters in all three books made choices that showed they cared about each other. Invite children to create a "Caring Constellation" as a reminder that we *all* have the ability to shine brightly and show we care. Have children draw several large stars, hearts, and polka dots, and write or draw words, sentences, or pictures on them that reflect caring. Give examples: "I can make a difference." "I can be a good friend." "Everyone deserves to be treated with kindness." Have children cut out their shapes and mount them on a black bulletin board or poster board to create a "Caring Constellation." Alternately, have them add the shapes to mobiles to hang up at home or school.

Series Activity: What Comes Next?

Weird! Dare! Tough! . . . what comes next? Ask children to imagine and make predictions about what happens to the characters in the next book. Encourage them to consider the main characters: *Luisa, Jayla,* and *Sam,* as well as the peripheral characters in the books: *Emily, Thomas, Patrick, Will, Mr. C.,* and *Alex.* Then have kids create and present their own book title and storyboard.

About the Author and Illustrator

Erin Frankel has a master's degree in English education and is passionate about teaching and writing. She taught ESL in Alabama before moving to Madrid, Spain, with her husband Alvaro and their three daughters, Gabriela, Sofia, and Kelsey. Erin knows firsthand what it feels like to be bullied, and she hopes her stories will help bring smiles back to children who have been involved in bullying. She and her longtime friend and illustrator Paula Heaphy share the belief that all children have the right to feel safe, loved, and confident in who they are. In her free time, Erin loves hiking in the Spanish mountains with her puppy Bella, as well as kayaking in her hometown of Mays Landing, New Jersey, which she visits as often as she can.

Paula Heaphy is a print and pattern designer in the fashion industry. She's an explorer of all artistic mediums from glassblowing to shoemaking, but her biggest love is drawing. She jumped at the chance to illustrate her friend Erin's story, having been bullied herself as a child. As the character of Luisa came to life on paper, Paula felt her path in life suddenly shift into focus. She lives in Brooklyn, New York, where she hopes to use her creativity to light up the hearts of children for years to come.

The Weird Series

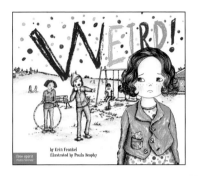

by Erin Frankel, illustrated by Paula Heaphy. 48 pp. Ages 5–9.

More Great Books from Free Spirit

Bystander Power
by Phyllis Kaufman Goodstein and Elizabeth Verdick, illustrated by Steve Mark
128 pp. Ages 8–13.

Bullies Are a Pain in the Brain
written and illustrated by Trevor Romain
112 pp. Ages 8–13.

Cliques, Phonies, & Other Baloney
written and illustrated by Trevor Romain
136 pp. Ages 8–13.

Good-Bye Bully Machine
by Debbie Fox and Allan L. Beane, Ph.D., illustrated by Debbie Fox
48 pp. Ages 8 & up.

Interested in purchasing multiple quantities and receiving volume discounts?
Contact edsales@freespirit.com or call 1.800.735.7323 and ask for Education Sales.

Many Free Spirit authors are available for speaking engagements, workshops, and keynotes.
Contact speakers@freespirit.com or call 1.800.735.7323.

For pricing information, to place an order, or to request a free catalog, contact:

free spirit PUBLISHING®

217 Fifth Avenue North • Suite 200 • Minneapolis, MN 55401-1299 • toll-free 800.735.7323 • local 612.338.2068
fax 612.337.5050 • help4kids@freespirit.com • www.freespirit.com